What Is Democracy?

UNDERSTANDING CITIZENSHIP

Dale Dixon

CiViCS FOR THE REAL WORLD™

Rosen Classroom™

Think about the United States. You might think of freedom, the flag, or an eagle. You might also think of democracy.

The word "democracy" comes from two Greek words. *Demos* means "the people" and *kratos* means "rule."

Can you guess what "democracy" means? It's a government ruled by the people!

In a democracy, everyone has a say in how the government is run. The people help make the rules.

Democracy began in Greece. The Greeks had democracy more than 2,000 years ago!

The United States has a representative democracy. Representatives are people who speak for other people.

There are a lot of people in the United States. They vote for people to represent, or speak for them, in the government.

Representatives make laws that the people want. Their job is to listen to the people.

If representatives don't do what the people want, they could lose their jobs. The people will vote for new representatives.

Think about democracy the next time you look at the flag. Democracy makes the United States a great country.

WORDS TO KNOW

eagle

flag

Greece

representative